THE U.S. CIVIL WAR ON THE FRONT LINES

by Tim Cooke

CAPSTONE PRESS
a capstone imprint

Edge Books are published by Capstone Press,
1710 Roe Crest Drive, North Mankato, Minnesota 56003
www.capstonepub.com

Published in 2014 by Capstone Publishers, Ltd.

Copyright © 2014 Brown Bear Books Ltd.
All rights reserved. No part of this book may be reproduced, stored in a retrieval system, or transmitted in any form or by any means, electronic, mechanical, photocopying, recording, or otherwise, without the prior written permission of the copyright holder.

Library of Congress Cataloging-in-Publication Data

The U.S. Civil War on the front lines / by Tim Cooke.
    pages cm. -- (Edge books. Life on the front lines)
Includes bibliographical references and index.
Summary: "Approaches the topic of the Civil War from the perspective of those fighting in it"-- Provided by publisher.
ISBN 978-1-4914-0842-1 (library binding) -- ISBN 978-1-4914-0848-3 (pbk.)
1. United States--History--Civil War, 1861-1865--Juvenile literature.
2. United States--History--Civil War, 1861-1865--Social aspects--Juvenile literature. 3. Soldiers--United States--History--19th century--Juvenile literature. 4. Soldiers--Confederate States of America--Juvenile literature. I. Title.
E468.C773 2015
973.7'1--dc23

2013049463

For Brown Bear Books Ltd:
Editorial Director: Lindsey Lowe
Text: Tim Cooke
Children's Publisher: Anne O'Daly
Design Manager: Keith Davis
Designer: Lynne Lennon
Picture Manager: Sophie Mortimer
Production Director: Alastair Gourlay

Source Notes
p.8 Robert E. Lee, Recollections and Letters of Robert E. Lee, Cosimo Classics, 2008, p.26 (originally published 1904); p.11 Oliver Norton, quoted in William C. Davis, Fighting Men of the Civil War, Salamander Books, 1998, p38; p.13 Ulysees S. Grant, quoted in Buck T. Foster, Sherman's Mississippi Campaign, University of Alabama Press, 2006, p.9; p.17 Tilton C. Reynolds, from www.loc.gov/collection/tilton-c-reynolds-papers/; p.19 John D. Billings, from Hardtack and Coffee: Or the Unwritten Story of Army Life, Bison Books, 1993, p.122; p.21 Amanda Aiken, from www.americanhistory.si.edu/documentsgallery/exhibitions/nursing_4.html; p.23 James Longstreet, from www.eyewitnesstohistory.com/pickettscharge.htm; p.27 John McCreery, from McCreery Letters, John Sickles Collection, U.S. Army Military History Institute, Carlisle, Pennsylvania; p.29 Sam Watkins, quoted in Benjamin Albert Botkin (ed.), A Civil War Treasury of Tales, Legends and Folklore, First Bison Books, 2000, p.73.

Photo Credits
Front Cover: Library of Congress
All interior images: Library of Congress: 5tr, 9tr, 9bl, 10, 11t, 12, 13tl, 15, 17tl, 17bl, 18/19, 19tl, 22, 23tr, 23bl, 25cr, 26/27, 27br, 29br; National Archives and Records Administration: 4/5, 6/7, 7t, 8, 11b, 13b, 14, 16, 19br, 21tl, 21b, 24/25, 26b, 28/29, 28b.
Artistic effects: Shutterstock

All Artworks © Brown Bear Books Ltd
Brown Bear Books has made every attempt to contact the copyright holder. If you have any information please contact smortimer@windmillbooks.co.uk

Printed in China

TABLE OF CONTENTS

The Civil War 4

The Making of a Soldier 6
    Recruitment and the Draft 8
    Training 10
    Transportation 12

At the Front 14
    Living Conditions 16
    Food and Drink 18
    Medicine and Health 20
    Under Fire 22

Spirit and Morale 24
    Keeping in Touch 26
    Recreation 28

Glossary 30
Read More 31
Internet Sites 31
Index 32

THE CIVIL WAR

The election of Abraham Lincoln as U.S. president in November 1860 brought to a head deep divisions in the United States. Like many Northerners, Lincoln wished to abolish slavery in the South. Southerners were determined to preserve their way of life. Six states left the Union and created the Confederate States of America. Five more states joined them later. Lincoln went to war to force them to remain in the Union.

The 8th New York State Militia pose for a photo. They were among the early volunteers at the start of the war.

Although there were relatively few large-scale battles during the Civil War, those that were fought were very costly. Modern rifles and cannons caused huge damage to soldiers and property.

Both sides believed the conflict would be short. It soon became clear that it would be long and bloody. The North's plan was to cut off and divide the South. The South planned to invade the North and force it to negotiate peace.

The conflict began well for the Confederates, who gained significant victories in 1861 and 1862. By 1863, however, the tide was turning. Under General Ulysses S. Grant, Union troops turned back a Southern advance at Gettysburg. They also captured the city of Vicksburg, Mississippi, leaving the Union in control of the Mississippi River. The South now faced a struggle to supply its troops with food and arms. After fighting on for over a year, the Confederate commander Robert E. Lee surrendered to Grant in April 1865.

CHAPTER 1

THE MAKING OF A SOLDIER

At the start of the Civil War in 1861, the Union Army was only 16,000 men strong. No organized Confederate army even existed. When war began, President Abraham Lincoln ordered a recruitment drive in the Union. He called for 75,000 men to serve for 90 days. About 91,000 men volunteered.

In the South the Confederate Army was created from nothing. Many of its officers had served in the U.S. Army, but resigned so they could serve the South.

Union soldiers line up for parade at an army camp. The officers are at the front. The ordinary soldiers are arranged in rows behind them.

Like the North, the Confederacy originally called for volunteers to enlist for 12 months. Later in the war, both sides introduced a form of **draft**. Able-bodied men were forced into military service. Beginning in 1862, African-Americans were allowed to join the Union Army. Many were eager to fight to help end slavery.

By the end of the war, 1.5 million men from the Union had served in the Civil War. In the Confederacy the number stood at just over 1 million.

Union private D.W.C. Arnold poses with his rifle and pack in front of a cannon. Many of the soldiers who joined the armies were farmers or small businessmen. Most had rarely been away from home before they joined the military.

- **draft:** a system of selecting men for compulsory service in the army

RECRUITMENT AND THE DRAFT

The Union Army had 35,000 soldiers by July 1861. Most of them were untrained volunteers. The Confederate Army commanded by General Pierre G.T. Beauregard had 20,000 men. Men on both sides were motivated to join by their belief in the cause. Some joined to claim the **bounty** volunteers received. As the war went on, it became more difficult to recruit volunteers. Both sides forced men into military service. This was unpopular. There were riots against the draft in New York City in July 1863.

A young Union drummer from the 22nd New York Infantry poses against a tree.

EYEWITNESS
Name: Robert E. Lee
Rank: General, Confederate Army

"With all my devotion to the Union and the feeling of loyalty and duty of an American citizen, I have not been able to make up my mind to raise my hand against my relatives, my children, my home."

8

These drawings from a New York City newspaper show the recruitment of soldiers in the city in August 1861. The scenes show Union officers helping recruits sign up before marching away with them.

This poster seeks to attract Union recruits. It offers volunteers regular pay, clothing, food, and somewhere to live. It also promises state and federal bounties, both on enlisting and at the end of the war.

- **bounty:** a payment of money made by the state in return for a service

TRAINING

The recruits had to learn basic skills quickly. They drilled for hours. The drills taught them how to line up in rows and march in columns and how to load their rifles. Soldiers repeated the movements so often that they became automatic, even in battle.

On the battlefield, infantrymen fought in rows, as they had in the American Revolution. But new weapons such as rifles caused heavy casualties, so commanders changed **tactics**. Soldiers began to fight in small loose groups.

New Union recruits hold a parade in a training camp. Regular drill enabled groups of men to move around together in battle.

- **tactic:** a plan and method used by commanders to position and move their men in battle

New recruits arrive at Camp Curtin in Harrisburg, Pennsylvania. Most training was organized by states, and each state was required to send a certain number of troops to the armies.

EYEWITNESS
NAME: Oliver Norton
RANK: Private, 83rd Pennsylvania Infantry Regiment

"The first thing in the morning is drill, then drill, then drill again. Then drill, drill, a little more drill. Then drill, and lastly drill. Between drills, we drill and sometimes stop to eat a little and have roll-call."

Units known as Zouaves based their appearance on that of French troops in North Africa.

TRANSPORTATION

The Civil War was the first war in which the railroad played a big part. Steam trains carried Southern troops to the first battle of the war at Bull Run, Virginia. Destroying railroads was a key aim for the South.

Cavalry on both sides used horses for transportation. Horses also pulled artillery weapons and supply carts. For most infantrymen, however, moving around meant marching for miles at a time.

A paddle steamer approaches a Union supply depot. Ships carried troops and supplies. Rivers became important highways for the competing armies.

12

Most of the time, armies moved on foot. In this drawing, two columns of Union infantry meet after leaving their transport ships.

EYEWITNESS
Name: Ulysses S. Grant
Rank: Union General
Place: Vicksburg, Mississippi, when giving orders in May 1863

"Collect stores and **forage**, and destroy the river railroad bridge and the road as far east as possible, as well as north and south."

The North had far more miles of railroad than the South, giving it a clear advantage.

- **cavalry:** troops that fight on horseback
- **forage:** food that is gathered from the surroundings, particularly fodder for animals

13

CHAPTER 2

AT THE FRONT

After basic training, a soldier was ready to fight. Most troops saw only a few major battles, such as Gettysburg, but many **skirmishes**. There were also **sieges** and campaigns of destruction Soldiers marched for miles in worn-out uniforms, sleeping on the road. Soldiers had to carry all of their possessions. They faced long hours of drill. There was widespread disease in army camps.

Wounded soldiers rest under trees after fighting at Marye's Heights, Virginia, in 1863. Lightly wounded men were returned to active service as soon as possible.

Soldiers were often hungry. In the South, Confederate soldiers could rely on local people to feed them. Union soldiers had some rations, but when these rations ran out they bought expensive food from merchants.

When men were not marching or fighting, they were bored. They spent hours and hours playing cards, making music, or writing and reading letters. As the war progressed, **desertion** became an increasing problem. Many soldiers felt they should be at home, helping their families with farms or businesses.

Under fire, Union forces cross the Rappahannock River to Fredericksburg in December 1862.

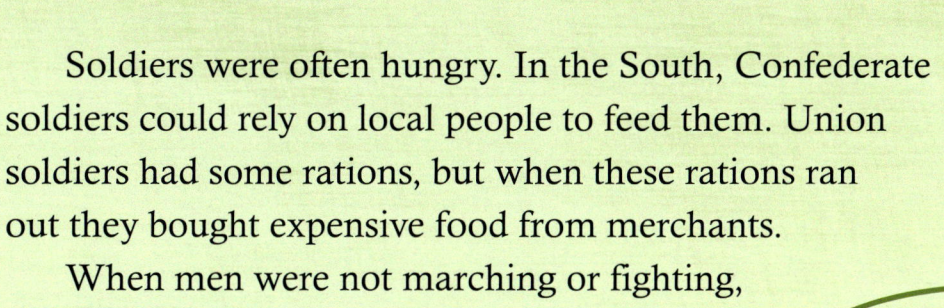

- **skirmish:** a clash between groups of soldiers
- **siege:** an operation where a position is surrounded and forced to surrender
- **desertion:** leaving the army without permission

LIVING CONDITIONS

Soldiers on both sides usually slept in canvas tents. Union camps consisted of rows of what the soldiers called "dog tents," because they said they were more suitable for a dog than a human. Each soldier was allocated half a tent. Officer and hospital tents were bigger. Confederate soldiers, who had no standard tent, seized dog tents if they got the chance. In winter soldiers moved to log cabins for shelter. Cabins were warmer and better at keeping out snow and mud.

Union soldiers pose outside their winter quarters.

These cabins were built as Confederate winter quarters at Manassas, which Northerners called Bull Run.

EYEWITNESS
Name: Tilton C. Reynolds
Unit: 105th Pennsylvania Infantry Regiment

"The tents are made of heavy bag stuff and there is no rain can get in. We can tie them shut and live as nice as you please."

An African-American soldier sits outside his military camp tent. African-Americans could join the Union Army starting in late 1862, but they often faced racial prejudice from their white officers and their fellow soldiers.

17

FOOD AND DRINK

Union soldiers usually received **rations**, such as salted pork and hardtack. Hardtack were tasteless, hard flour biscuits nicknamed "tooth-dullers." Soldiers sliced their pork over the hardtack to soften it. For a treat, they ate beef and baked beans. Their rations also included coffee beans to roast and grind. Sutlers sold luxuries such as butter and cookies.

Southerners did not receive rations. They ate whatever they could get from civilians or from the land. Their staples were dishes such as molasses, peas, cornmeal, and rice. They had to make do with a coffee substitute instead of the real thing.

A freed slave serves dinner to Union officers at Brandy Station, Virginia.

- **ration:** a limited amount of types of food or drink that is distributed to everyone equally

Union soldiers cook food at their camp. When units had no official cook, the men took turns preparing food.

EYEWITNESS
Name: John D. Billings
Unit: 10th Massachusetts Volunteer Artillery

"What a godsend it [coffee] was to us! How often after being completely jaded by a night march have I had a wash, if there was water to be had, made and drunk my pint or so of coffee and felt as fresh and invigorated as if just arisen from a night's sound sleep."

In camp soldiers could get food at a company kitchen, like this log hut, which served food to Union soldiers.

MEDICINE AND HEALTH

Doctors in the 1860s knew little of bacteria and germs or of how diseases spread. More soldiers died from disease than died on the battlefield. Military camps often had poor **hygiene**. They were breeding grounds for diseases, such as chicken pox and measles. Diseases spread rapidly in such cramped conditions. Men often died from their illnesses. Sometimes patients were given whiskey, brandy, or coffee to provide them some comfort.

Wounded soldiers recover in the Carver General Hospital in Washington, D.C. The nurses were all civilian volunteers.

A Union surgeon, or "sawbones," operates outside a hospital tent. Without antibiotics, many patients died from infection.

EYEWITNESS
NAME: Amanda Akin
OCCUPATION: Volunteer Nurse
PLACE: Armory Square Hospital, New York City

"Oh dear me, the cry is 'Still they come' and we are overflowing; they come now without any order, and are received with but little ceremony."

Lines of Union ambulances wait to retrieve wounded men from the battlefield.

- **hygiene:** the degree to which people keep themselves or their surrounding clean, especially to avoid disease

21

UNDER FIRE

The Civil War was the first time **rifled** weapons were widely used. They fired farther and more accurately than previous weapons. The Springfield rifle was the standard infantry weapon. Its lead bullets caused terrible wounds, and many soldiers bled to death. The fighting was often at short range, such as when soldiers fought hand-to-hand with bayonets. Artillery fire was another danger, especially during a siege. The besiegers were positioned around a city. From there, they rained shells on the soldiers and civilians trapped inside the city.

Union troops attack Confederate positions during the Battle of Spotsylvania.

EYEWITNESS

Name: James Longstreet
Rank: Confederate General
Place: Gettysburg, 1863

"As I rode, the shells screaming over my head and ploughing the ground under my horse, an involuntary appeal went up that one of them might take me from scenes of such awful responsibility."

Union forces attack Confederate positions at the Battle of Antietam in Maryland in September 1862.

Confederates shell Union forces in Fort Sumter, North Carolina. The attack on the fort sparked the start of the war.

- **rifled:** having spiraled grooves inside the barrel of a gun to make bullets travel more accurately

23

CHAPTER 3

SPIRIT AND MORALE

On both sides of the conflict, men at first eagerly enlisted to support their respective cause. Nearly everyone believed the campaign would soon be over. But as the war dragged on, **morale** fell, and it became harder to recruit new soldiers. News of a battlefield defeat or victory affected the spirits of soldiers hundreds of miles away. Many people were tired of the war.

Union prisoners of war enjoy a game of baseball at Salisbury Prison in North Carolina.

Despite falling morale, both sides believed that they had to fight on. In the 1864 Union presidential election, 80 percent of soldiers voted for Lincoln and the continuation of the war, as opposed to only 53 percent of civilians.

Confederate morale was usually high. The Confederate soldiers believed they were fighting to preserve the Southern lifestyle against a threat from the North. It was only late in the war, when their cause was hopeless, that Confederate morale declined and soldiers began to desert in large numbers.

The Confederate 3rd Arkansas Infantry parade with their musicians in 1861. Even if units did not have a band, they had at least a drummer and a fifer to provide music to keep up spirits.

- **morale:** the fighting spirit of a person or group, and how confident they feel of winning a victory

25

KEEPING IN TOUCH

For homesick soldiers, the mail was a lifeline. Men on both sides spent their free time writing home. The arrival of the mail wagon at camp was cause for celebration. If it came late, men got angry. Families also sent care packages containing baked goods, socks, shirts, soaps, and other home comforts. Soldiers would keep and reread their letters. Many men also kept a pocket diary of the conflict.

Union troops rest after drill in 1864. Some play cards, while others read letters or newspapers.

A group of Union officers in Culpeper, Virginia, read letters from home outside their tent.

A Union soldier finds a private place to read a letter from home.

EYEWITNESS
NAME: John McCreery
RANK: Private, 6th North Carolina Regiment
PLACE: First Battle of Bull Run
(McCreery's own spelling in a letter)

"Sutch a day the booming of the cannon ratling of the muskets you have no idea how it was I have turned threw that old book of yours and looked at the pictures and read a little about war but I did not no anything what it was."

RECREATION

When soldiers were not marching or fighting, they kept boredom at bay by writing letters or diaries. They also played cards and horseshoes or read newspapers. Some men kept pets—mainly dogs, but also cats, raccoons, and even squirrels. Many men enjoyed singing or playing fiddles, guitars, and banjos. Soldiers also played team games, including the new sport of baseball. Holidays were celebrated in camp with feasts, foot races, horse racing, music, and boxing matches. When soldiers were really bored, they even raced lice against one another.

Regimental drum and fife corps accompanied soldiers into battle to keep their spirits high.

A Catholic chaplain carries out a mass for members of the 69th New York Militia in their camp at Fort Corcoran near Washington, D.C.

EYEWITNESS
NAME: Sam Watkins, Confederate soldier
PLACE: Tupelo, Mississippi

"There was one fellow who was winning all the money; his lice would run quicker and crawl faster than anybody's lice. We could not understand it. The lice were placed in plates—this was the race course—and the first that crawled off was the winner. At last we found out his trick; he always heated the plate."

Union soldiers play cards outside their tents. Many soldiers gambled heavily. Some owed their entire monthly pay to other soldiers before receiving it.

GLOSSARY

bounty (BOWN-tee)—a payment of money made by the state in return for a service

cavalry (KA-vul-ree)—soldiers who fight on horseback

draft (DRAFT)—a system of selecting men for compulsory service in the army

desertion (dee-ZUHR-shuhn)—leaving the army without permission

forage (FOr-ij)—food that is gathered from the surroundings, particularly fodder for animals

hygiene (HYE-jeen)—the degree to which people keep themselves or their surrounding clean, especially to avoid disease

morale (muh-RAL)—the fighting spirit of a person or group, and how confident they feel of winning a victory

ration (RAH-shun)—a limited amount of food or drink that is distributed to everyone equally

rifled (RYE-fuhld)—having spiraled grooves inside the barrel of a gun to make bullets travel more accurately

siege (SEEJ)—an operation where a position is surrounded and forced to surrender

skirmish (SKIR-mish)—a brief clash between small groups of soldiers

tactic (TAK-tik)—a way in which commanders position and move their men in battle

READ MORE

Beller, Susan Provost. *Billy Yank and Johnny Reb: Soldiering in the Civil War.* Minneapolis: Twenty-First Century Books, 2007.

Kent, Zachary. *The Civil War: From Fort Sumter to Appomattox.* The United States at War. Berkeley Heights, NJ: Enslow Publishing, Inc., 2011.

Kreiser, Lawrence A., and Ray B. Browne. *Voices of Civil War America: Contemporary Accounts of Daily Life.* Voices of an Era. Santa Barbara, Calif.: Greenwood, 2011.

Ratliff, Thomas. *You Wouldn't Want to Be a Civil War Soldier!: A War You'd Rather Not Fight.* New York: Franklin Watts, 2013.

Samuels, Charlie. *Timeline of the Civil War.* Americans at War. New York: Gareth Stevens Publishing, 2012.

Stanchak, John E. *Eyewitness Civil War.* New York: DK Publishing, 2011.

INTERNET SITES

FactHound offers a safe, fun way to find Internet sites related to this book. All of the sites on FactHound have been researched by our staff.

Here's all you do:

Visit www.facthound.com

Type in this code: 9781491408421

Check out projects, games and lots more at www.capstonekids.com

INDEX

African-Americans, 7

Beauregard, P.G.T., 8
bounty, 8

cabins, 16
care packages, 26
cavalry, 12
coffee, 18
communications, 26–27

desertion, 15, 25
diaries, 26, 28
disease, 20
draft, 7, 8
draft riots, 8
drill, 10

food, 15, 18–19
    hardtack, 18
front line, 14–15

Gettysburg, Battle of, 5
Grant, Ulysses, S., 5

holidays, 28
homesickness, 14, 26
hygiene, 20

infantry, 10, 12, 22

Lee, Robert E., 5
letters, 26, 28
Lincoln, Abraham, 4, 6, 25
living conditions, 16–17

mail, 26
medicine, 20–21
morale, 24–25
music, 28

New York City, 8

pets, 28

railroads, 12
rations, 18
recreation, 28–29
recruitment, 6–7, 24

sieges, 14, 22
skirmishes, 14
slavery, 4, 7
Springfield rifles, 22

tactics, 10
tents, 16
training, 10–11
transportation, 12–13

Vicksburg, Mississippi, 5
volunteers, 7, 8

weapons, 22
    artillery, 22
    bayonets, 22
    Springfield rifles, 22